10 LITTLE MONSTERS *visit* OREGON

RICK WALTON

ILLUSTRATIONS BY JESS SMART SMILEY

GREETINGS FROM

OREGON

For Edwin Markham, poet laureate of Oregon. He drew a circle that took us in.

—RW

This book is for you.
(You know who you are.)

—JSS

Published by Familius™ LLC, www.familius.com

Familius books are available at special discounts for bulk purchases for sales promotions, family or corporate use. Special editions, including personalized covers, excerpts of existing books, or books with corporate logos, can be created in large quantities for special needs. For more information, contact Premium Sales at 559-876-2170 or email specialmarkets@familius.com.

Library of Congress Catalog-in-Publication Data
2014940270
ISBN 978-1-939629-29-6

Printed in China

Book and jacket design by David Miles

10 9 8 7 6 5 4 3 2 1
First Edition

10 Little Monsters, looking for fun,
Take a trip to Oregon!

10 Little Monsters, they can't wait,
'Cause monsters LOVE the Beaver State!

10

Little Monsters say, “Look there!
Pictures rising in the air!”
Up they go. They have a great time
’Til one remembers that . . .

The Astoria Column is a 125-foot-tall column that stands on a 600-foot-tall hill in Astoria, Oregon. The outside of the column is covered in murals depicting the early history of Oregon. If you visit the column, try climbing it on the inside, where the steps are.

. . . he can't climb.

9 Little Monsters love Tillamook cheese.
"We would like free samples, please!"

The Tillamook Cheese Factory makes cheese, butter, yogurt, sour cream, and ice cream, and sells them in all 50 states.

One monster trips while looking for lunch.

New ice cream flavor: *Monster Crunch*.

Tillamook ice cream is quality checked to make sure that no monsters have fallen into it.

8 Little Monsters stick their noses
In thousands and thousands of beautiful roses.
One Little Monster is picked and bought.

"He loves me . . . he loves me not."
The Portland Rose Festival is a huge annual event that includes parades, Navy ships, fireworks, carnival rides, and dragon boat races. And of course, lots and lots and LOTS of flowers.

7 Little Monsters love to read.

Powell's Books has just what they need.

Powell's Books, with its 4 million new and used books, is the largest independent bookstore in the world. 3,999,999 of its books do not have a monster smashed inside.

One Little Monster reads all day . . .

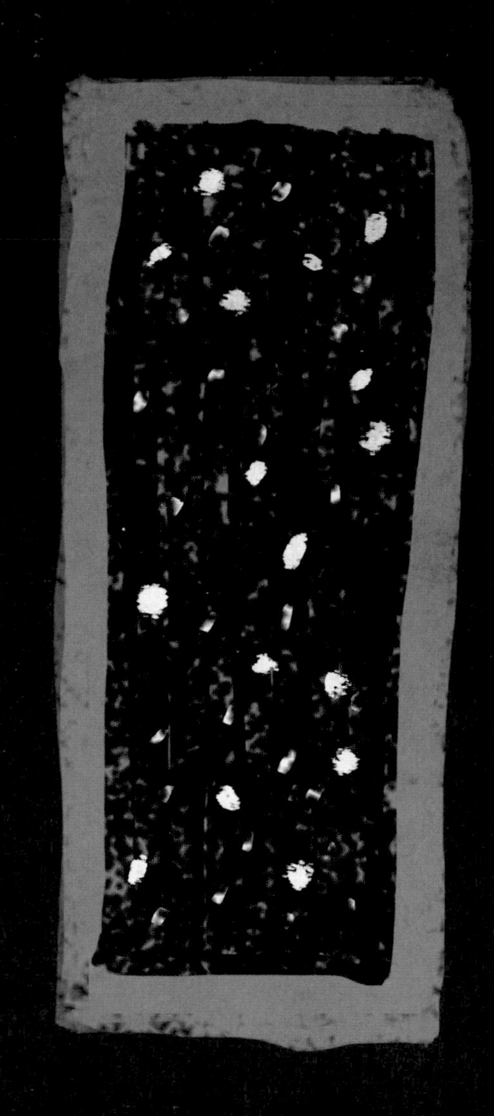

'Til the book is closed and put away.

6 Little Monsters play hide-and-seek
Up and down an Oregon creek.
One stays quiet and still all day . . .

The beaver was so important to the early Oregon economy that Oregon is known as "The Beaver State." Though beavers do chew down trees (and, apparently, monsters), don't worry. As far as we know, a beaver has never been known to chew down a person.

'Til a beaver chews him
and hauls him away.

5 Little Monsters like to eat bugs.
Their favorite treat? Banana slugs.

Pick them up and chew, chew, chew.

But banana slugs like monsters, too!

The banana slug—which does, indeed, look somewhat like a banana—is one of the largest slugs in the world. It dries out easily, which is why it likes damp places like Oregon. Though banana slugs think monsters taste delicious, they think you taste disgusting. You would probably feel the same about them. Banana slugs are not technically bugs, but what do monsters know?

4

Little Monsters sing in the sea,

"Come, little sea lions! Play with me!"

The monsters have no fun at all.

The sea lions, though, they have a ball!

Sea Lion Caves is America's largest sea cave. It is home to sea lions and sea birds. Sea monsters, however, are not allowed.

Little Monsters take a break

To do some wading at Crater Lake.

"Looks shallow enough. How deep can it be?"

One Little Monster says, "I'll see."

Crater Lake, made by a volcano, is almost 2,000 feet deep—the deepest lake in the United States. Unless you are very, very tall, you should not try to wade across it.

Little Monsters spend all day
At an all-you-can-eat fungus buffet.
One monster says, “I’ll eat just one.”

But he explodes before he's done.

The world's largest living organism is the Armillaria solidipes fungus beneath the Malheur National Forest in Oregon. It is 2,200 acres large and 2,400 years old. Don't try to harvest it unless you have a really big truck.

1 Little Monster decides to go . . .

To ride and rope in a rodeo.

He can’t hold on. See him fly!

Poor Little Monster. Wave goodbye!

The Pendleton Round-Up is one of the top rodeos in the world. Held in September each year, the week-long celebration of western heritage also includes parades, concerts, and other fun events. No monster has ever won a Pendleton rodeo event.